WANTED: THE PERFECT PET

Fiona Roberton

G. P. Putnam's Sons • An Imprint of Penguin Group (USA) Inc.

No ducks were harmed in the making of this book.

For Henry, Olivia and Anna.

WANTED: THE PERFECT PET

Fiona Roberton

G. P. Putnam's Sons • An Imprint of Penguin Group (USA) Inc.

G. P. PUTNAM'S SONS ● A division of Penguin Young Readers Group.
Published by The Penguin Group. Penguin Group (USA) Inc., 375 Hudson Street, New York, NY 10014, U.S.A. Penguin Group
(Canada), 90 Eglinton Avenue East, Suite 700, Toronto, Ontario M4P 2Y3, Canada (a division of Pearson Penguin Canada
Inc.). Penguin Books Ltd, 80 Strand, London WC2R 0RL, England. Penguin Ireland, 25 St. Stephen's Green, Dublin 2,
Ireland (a division of Penguin Books Ltd.). Penguin Group (Australia), 250 Camberwell Road, Camberwell, Victoria 3124,
Australia (a division of Pearson Australia Group Pty Ltd). Penguin Books India Pvt Ltd, 11 Community Centre, Panchsheel
Park, New Delhi – 110 017, India. Penguin Group (NZ), 67 Apollo Drive, Rosedale, North Shore 0632, New Zealand
(a division of Pearson New Zealand Ltd). Penguin Books (South Africa) (Pty) Ltd, 24 Sturdee Avenue, Rosebank,
Johannesburg 2196, South Africa. Penguin Books Ltd, Registered Offices: 80 Strand, London WC2R 0RL, England.

Manufactured in China.

Library of Congress Cataloging-in-Publication Data
Roberton, Fiona. Wanted: the perfect pet / Fiona Roberton.—1st American ed. p. cm. Summary: A boy who desperately wants a pet dog
ends up with a duck instead. [1. Ducks as pets—Fiction. 2. Dogs—Fiction. 3. Pets—Fiction.] I. Title. PZ7.R5393Wan 2010 [E]—dc22
2009037766

ISBN 978-0-399-25461-1
Special Markets ISBN 978-0-399-25565-6 Not for resale
1 3 5 7 9 10 8 6 4 2

Chapter 1
The Boy

- hello

Once upon a time there lived a boy named Henry.

What Henry wanted more than
anything else in the whole wide world,

more than chips,

more than a cowboy costume,

more than an all-expenses-paid
trip to the moon,

more, even, than
world peace itself,

was a Dog.

HARRY

LARRY

GARY

BOB

KENT

BARRY

JEFF

PEDRO

DAVE

IAIN

MIKE

ERIC

Bu

RICH

KYLIE

GEORGE

BRUCE

etc.

"But Henry," said his mother,
"you already have 27 different varieties
of frog, surely they are enough?"

"No," said Henry sternly, "they are **boring**.

All they do is hop and **grrrribit**."

"I want a pet with **PERSONALITY.** I want a Dog.

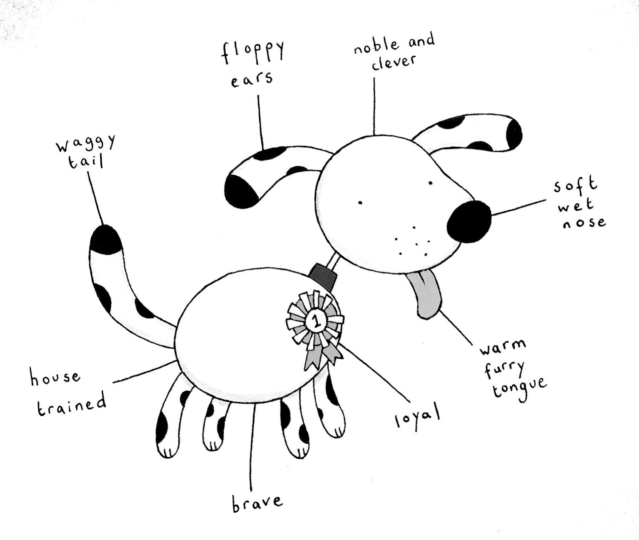

waggy tail

floppy ears

noble and clever

soft wet nose

house trained

warm furry tongue

loyal

brave

With floppy ears and a waggy tail,
and a soft wet nose, and a warm furry tongue.

A dog that can catch
balls that I throw,

that can learn
fantastic new tricks,

— SHAUSHIDGES

and that I can chase around trees.

Because it is common knowledge," said Henry,
"that a dog is The Perfect Pet for a boy."

So he decided to advertise.

FOR SALE:

TIME MACHINE
Settings include 'Iron Age', 'Medieval Times' and 'The Renaissance'. Requires 4xAA Batteries. Hours of fun for all the family. Parental supervision recommended. Ages 4+.
Call: 02 - 362 4716

FOR RENT:

CASTLE, TRANSYLVANIA
3284 bedrooms, 2 bathrooms, comfortable dungeons, roof terrace, atmosphere of impending doom, pit of evil, stunning views. Boobytrapped.
Call: 02 - 376 4716

FOR HIRE:

ANGRY MOB
Available for all occasions including weddings, political rallies and monster lynchings.
Call: 02 - 272 3345

WOODCUTTER
Own axe, willing to travel.
Call: 07 - 786 5491

X-RAY GOGGLES
Can see through walls, clothing, lies, space, and time.
Call: 06 - 903 2672

WANTED:
THE PERFECT PET

ALSO KNOWN AS A DOG
Must have waggy tail, floppy ears, soft wet nose and warm furry tongue. Should be able to learn fantastic new tricks. Preferably house trained.
Apply in person to: Mr. Henry, The Pond House, 24 Tadpole Lane, Little Gribblington.
Or call: 01 - 362 2341
(Evenings and weekends only).

FOR FREE:

ENCHANTED MIRROR
Always speaks the truth.
Free to good home.
Call: 09 - 782 9101

FOR SALE:

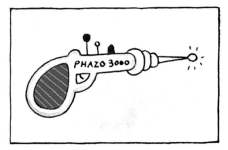

PHAZER GUN
Settings include 'Repel' and 'Stun'. Comfortable rubber grip, hair trigger, 12 metre range, anti-backfire mechanism. Package includes carry case, holster, targets and battery recharger. Ages 8+.
Call: 01 - 482 3761

And then he waited.

Chapter 2
The Duck

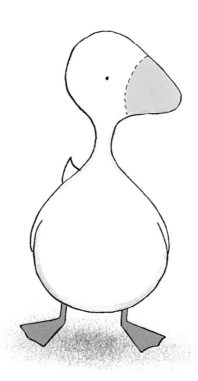

Once upon a time there lived a duck.
He didn't have a name.

He lived all alone, far, far away
at the top of a cold and windy hill.

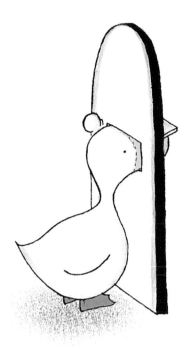

Nobody ever wrote.

Nobody ever called.

Nobody ever e-mailed.

He went to the movies,

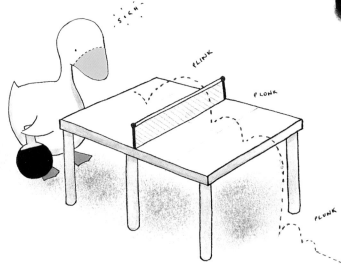

and played Ping-Pong,

and watched the sun rise, the sun float
about somewhere in the middle, and the sun
set, all by himself, every single day.

It wasn't much fun.

But then one day, he opened up his paper, and he saw:

"I am not a dog," he said, "but if I was a dog,
I could have a friend at last."

"A friend to have tea with, go to the movies with,
and play Ping-Pong with. A friend to watch the sun rise,
the sun float about somewhere in the middle,
and the sun set with."

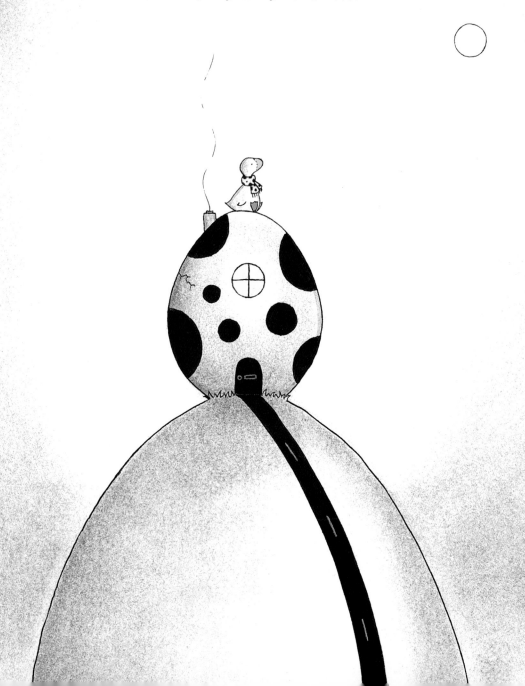

So with a pair of old socks, an egg box and some string,

perfect.

he created The Perfect Disguise.

Then he packed his things and set off on
the long journey to meet the boy.

Chapter 3
The Discovery

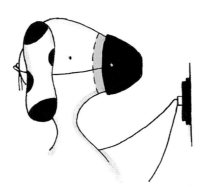

Ding-Dong!

"A Dog!"
yelled Henry.

"Woof!"
said the duck.

Henry had never been so excited.
The duck had never been happier. However...

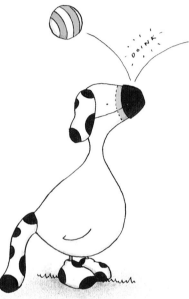

Henry's dog wasn't very
good at catching balls,

and he wasn't very good
at learning new tricks,

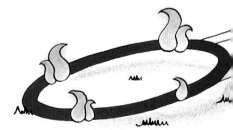

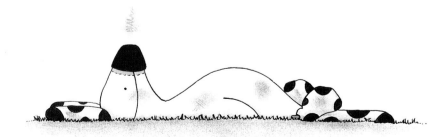

and when he chased Henry
around the trees,

he waddled...

and he slipped...

and he tripped...

and his soft wet nose and his
floppy ears and tail fell off.

Henry was stunned. The duck slowly stood up.
A single fat tear rolled down his beak and plopped
on the ground in front of him.

"I am sorry. I am not a dog,"
admitted the duck. "I am just a duck."

"I do not have floppy ears, or a waggy tail, or a soft wet nose, or even a warm furry tongue," he said sadly.

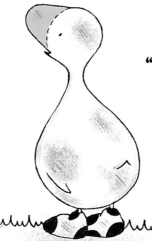

"Oh," said Henry disappointedly. "No, you don't."

Henry thought for a moment. Then he picked up the duck and carried him home.

He gave the duck a nice hot bath and a cup of tea.

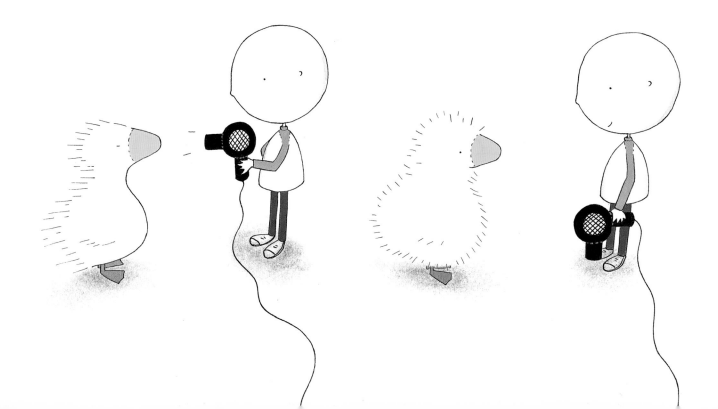

He took down his *Enormous Book of Incredibly Interesting Things,*

he looked under "D,"

and he made a list...

DUCK SKILLS

1. Can dive under water, can hold breath, swim and float on water. Fun in bath, at beach and useful for hunting for sunken treasure, fishing and fetching things I dropped in swimming pool.

2. Can 'FLY!' Could put on ~~aero~~ aeronautical show to earn extra pocket money. Also good skill for getting kites and frisbees and other items out of trees and next door's garden. And for drawing maps and spying on people.

3. This particular duck v.good at disguises = VERY CLEVER.

4. Nest building skills excellent for building forts and camps and tree houses and so on.

5. Spare feathers can be used to build indian headdresses and to tickle little sister with.

6. This duck can talk. Is rare, but not unheard of.

ALSO: Won't shed fur, get dog breath, need walking or house training. Won't eat homework, chew shoes or furniture, and won't pee on carpet.

↑ me   ↑ duck

...which he showed to the duck.

"So you might not be a dog," said Henry happily, "but you are certainly not JUST a duck. In fact, you might just be The Perfect Pet for me.

I think I'll call you Spot."
Henry smiled.

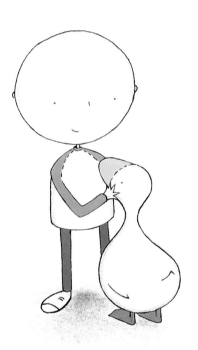

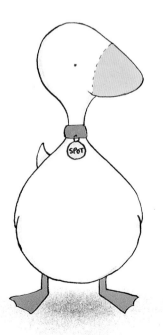

"Quack," said Spot.

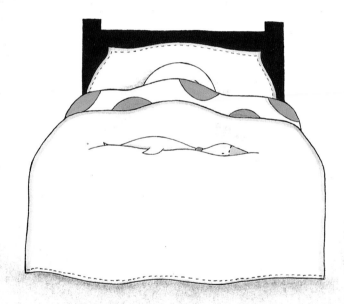

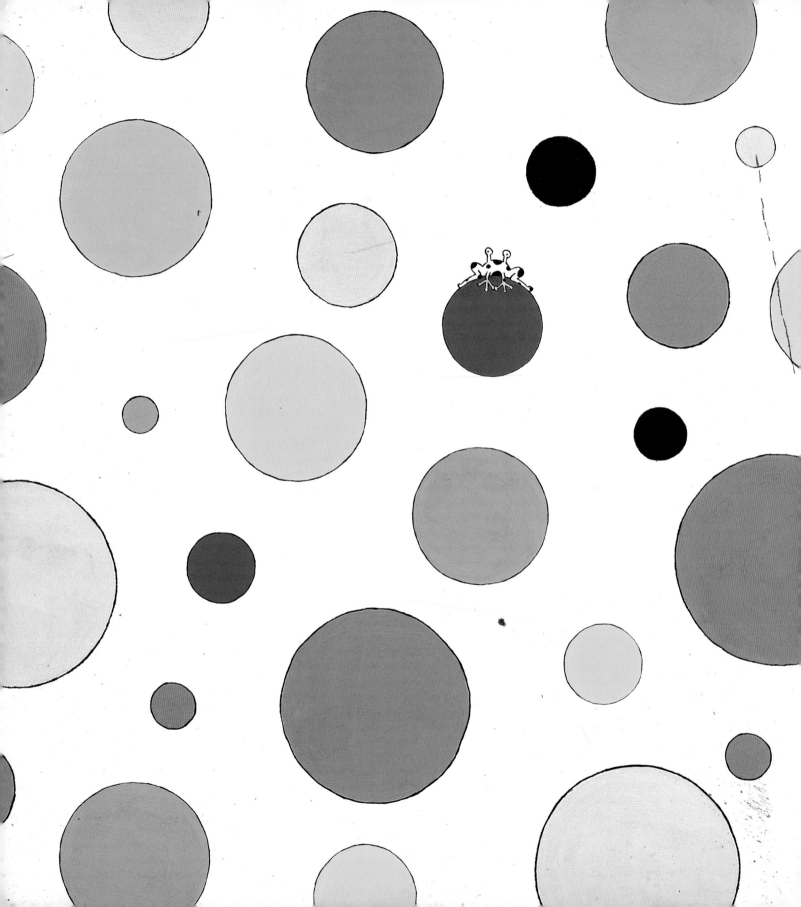